C000230101

JANE BETTELEY

These Thoughts Are Yours

A Collection of Short Stories

This book was professionally typeset on Reedsy.
Find out more at reedsy.com

For all of those who said I couldn't – I did. And for those who said I could – thank you.

Contents

Acknowledgement

This collection of short stories started life many years ago. I have always written, it is my way of making sense of the things that live in my head (of which there are many). As an over thinker, I have found that writing things down is not only a great therapy, but is also really enjoyable. I have battled with myself over many years about whether to publish these stories, but there were so many barriers (all self made) that stopped me. What if people laughed at me? What if my writing wasn't very good? What if no-one wanted to read them? At the age of 46 I realised that those barriers were not valid as they didn't really matter, and the only thing stopping me was myself. I also battled with the anxiety and paranoia of peri-menopause and with a little help from some HRT, I realised that I could do whatever I wanted, and what I really wanted to do was publish a book.

There are a plethora of themes running through the book, and I will be honest, there was no plan when it came to what each one would be about, other than they would be centred around the female experience. There are some that are light-hearted such as *Small Talk* and *Down The Aisles* and others that run much deeper. In particular, *The Wait* touches on mental illness and *Again* explores misplaced trust. I have had many conversations with people about some of the themes, gaining a privileged insight into people's personal lives. This was quite difficult at times as these were raw feelings and emotions that belong to people who I respect greatly. Your encouragement and support and most importantly, your approval was extremely important to me. Thank you for sharing your experiences with me.

The length of the stories vary greatly and some are super short, which is intentional. They are snapshots in time, brief insights into a moment in life. A lot of these stories will be relatable to a lot of people, and rather than end these snapshots with a resolution, I wanted to leave them open, to invite people to think about what may happen next. And also, let's be honest, sometimes a few minutes is all we have! Some of these stories will fit perfectly into busy life.

These Thoughts Are Yours will always be special to me and I hope that you enjoy reading it as much as I have enjoyed bringing it together. It has been a labour of love, spanning many years, and finally, it can breathe life. Also, I need to publish it before everyone gets fed up with me talking about it.

And now for some gushy stuff...
   I am extremely fortunate to be surrounded by people who are the most honest, loyal and supportive friends. In fear of sounding cliched, these wonderful people are the reason I found the courage to write all of these stories down and release them to whoever may wish to read them. I won't name you all, but you know who you are.
   There are lots and lots of people who have influenced my writing, whether they realise it or not, so to list them all would be an impossible task. But there are a few that I would like to mention by name.

I want to send a special thanks to my editor, Judith, who was the first 'stranger' to read my stories. Your words confirmed that it was indeed time to let the stories go. Thank you Judith for your encouragement.

To Kim, my cover designer, one of the best people that I know. Thank you for capturing the essence of my first publication with the most perfect response. You're the best. x

To Karen & Jodie, we met through circumstance and a mutual love of literature, and here we are, 13 years later. You two keep me sane, keep me strong and I will be forever grateful for our friendship.

To my people. You are the ones who make me feel like I am the best version of myself every single day. We laugh, we cry (not as much as I used to though thankfully), we raise each other up and we appreciate each other. I am so very lucky to have you all in my life. You have been there through all of the dramas, the celebrations and the days that seem impossible. You have added light to the dark times and sparkle to the good. I consider myself extremely fortunate that you are in my life.

To David, my world. The person who picked me up and dusted me off and made me believe anything is possible. I love you endlessly. x

And finally to my team, O, M & T - you inspire me (and drive me mad) every day. You are the reason for it all. Keep being brilliant. I love you. x

1

Happy Ever After

Sarah sat on the hard wooden pew and shuffled her cream satin shoes together as she swung her legs backwards and forwards. Her pink, ankle length dress felt scratchy and they had used hairspray in her hair which made it feel stiff and horrible. Isabelle, her older cousin, put her hand on Sarah's knee, exuding bossiness with a simple touch. She gave Sarah the death stare. Sarah sighed and stopped swinging her legs. She had never wanted to be a bridesmaid in the first place; it just wasn't her thing. She hadn't worn pink since she was old enough to verbally express that she thought pink was 'yukky'. 'You have to do what Aunty Becky wants, it's *her* day' her mother had told her on numerous occasions. Sarah really couldn't understand why she couldn't just be honest and say 'nah you're alright, I don't really want to be a bridesmaid' but her mother would tell her she was being difficult. Again.

The problem was, Sarah had never been what you would call girly, despite her blond curls and perfectly placed freckles. She always felt that boys had way more fun. They could play football and get muddy and no one would harp on about what a shame it was that she had gotten her pretty little face all dirty. She wanted to play army, marbles, wrestling, not Barbie dolls and hairdressers. She wanted to wear her joggers and her trainers, not frilly dresses and strappy shoes. The idea of having to parade around in that pink scratchy dress holding a posy of flowers was the last thing she wanted to do. Being a bridesmaid was absolutely her worst nightmare ever.

She strained her eyes to see across the pew, not daring to turn her head too much for fear of Isabelle and her hand of death. As her eyes darted over the faces and hats and suits she spotted Harry, sat like an angel, an angel who looked bored stiff. An involuntary smile appeared on her face and he caught her gaze, and smiled back with a simultaneously sympathetic and mischievous smile, his floppy blond hair spilling over his dark eyes. You didn't often see blond haired boys with dark eyes like Harry, but Harry was one of a kind. Sarah let her eyes wander further down the pew and saw Harry's mother and father sat very still, almost too still, their eyes glazed over and their faces stern. Not even a wedding could cheer them up or make them smile, thought Sarah. The sun beamed through the stained glass throwing jewels of light over their faces. At least they look pretty, she thought, even if they are miserable.

Harry pointed at his hair and mouthed 'your hair looks nice' and then put his hand over his mouth to contain his giggles. Sarah pulled a face at him, but discreetly, mindful that any wrong move would land her in serious trouble. Somehow Harry always managed to get away with things, and Sarah would be the one who got caught, the one who got punished. She didn't ever mind though, Harry had been through enough, she would rather take a telling off than risk Harry being upset. But Sarah couldn't risk it today, not at the wedding. Her Aunty Becky was lovely but boy could she hold a grudge. She still talked about the broken window pane on the side of her garage. It had got smashed during a rather boisterous game of cricket one unusually warm spring afternoon. Sarah recalled that Harry had had quite a bit of input in that situation too. Aunty Becky had phoned Sarah's mum, 'you've got to do something about her, she's out of control. She needs to take some responsibility for herself – she can't keep using Harry as an excuse'. It was always the same old story – they would always try and blame Harry.

It had been a really hot summer later that year, Sarah had spent quite a lot of time at the hospital talking to people in rooms with teddy bears and sofas and soft lighting. 'She needs some extra help' her mother would tell her friends, 'you know, after all that has gone on', and the friends would nod knowingly, not ever quite sure what to say. Sarah didn't need help; she needed everyone to just leave her alone and let her get on with it.

Harry got it, he understood - he never needed to ask her how she was feeling or tell her to talk to the teddy bear and explain what had happened. Harry often went to the hospital with her, but he used to make her laugh and her mum would get annoyed with her. The doctor would stare at Sarah and then write things down on his clipboard. 'You've got to stop' she would say to Harry, 'the doctor doesn't like it when I keep laughing at him'. Harry would look hurt for a second, but then that smile would appear and they'd just carry on as before. Harry had a habit of making her laugh when she wasn't supposed to. Just like now, as the choir started sing something churchy. Harry was miming along with the words, well not the actual words, just a 'la la la' type of singing, all lah-di-dah. Sarah stifled a giggle and looked to the floor. She loved the way Harry made her spark inside. She got so frustrated when people didn't understand. 'But he makes me so happy,' she would protest. But no one cared. No one wanted to listen, they just wanted her to stop talking about him.

After the choir had finished singing, Sarah dared to glance back over towards where Harry was sitting, but she couldn't find his face. Her eyes darted up and down the pews – she panicked slightly and turned her head right around to get a better view. Isabelle's ninja hand was there on her knee almost instantly. They've probably sent him away, she thought, her disappointment too much to conceal. Just as Sarah turned her head back to the front, Harry's mother, still stony faced and grey, caught her eye. They held a glance for a moment, until she broke away and dabbed at her eye with a well used handkerchief. Sarah turned away, her eyes fixed on the cold stone floor. Everyone was always so sad nowadays, even at a wedding, even now when Harry still made her laugh, everyone else was still so sad. If they would just get over it, if they would just try harder, they'd see he was happy, there was no need to be sad all of the time. It's not like Harry was sad, quite the opposite, Sarah had never seen him smile so much.

Sarah managed to hold it together quite well for the rest of the service, despite her bitter disappointment at Harry's disappearance. Without Harry's face she had nothing to laugh at, nothing to smile about. She tried to enjoy it, but it was no fun without him – she never had any fun without him. She managed to hold a smile long enough for the photos to be taken, although she had no idea why they needed to take so many. Her dress was still scratching the backs of her legs and her hair was starting to feel like it didn't belong to her. All she wanted to do was sit in the shade of the large oak tree in the middle of the graveyard with her best friend again. Harry loved trees.

The bride and groom were getting ready to leave for the reception. The brightly coloured wedding guests crowded around them with handfuls of confetti. Someone counted down from three and suddenly the sky was full of colours and shapes, all dancing on the breeze in a confusion of whether to fly or fall to the ground. There were whoops and cheers. It was so noisy, so many people, Sarah began to panic – the blur of colour and noise invading her thoughts like a thousand kites all battling for the same piece of sky. Her eyes darted across the churchyard in search of safety, in search of a friendly face, in search of Harry, but she still couldn't find him. Why did they always have to send him away? She felt her body tense and the tears collect in her eyes.

'What are you looking for?' a lady who Sarah had recognised from previous family occasions, clad in garish purple viscose and smelling of lavender had come behind her and put her hand on Sarah's shoulder. 'Harry' said Sarah. And there it was, the look – *that* look; a glance to someone else, a raising of eyebrows, a sympathetic smile. Sarah could feel the sick starting to rise in her throat. No one ever understood. Why did they look at her like this? She hated them. She hated the stupid wedding and she hated her stupid pink dress. She threw her flowers on the ground and ran as fast as she could, but her floor-length dress was not designed for running through churchyards. Her satin shoes caught in the hem and she fell forwards into the sun scorched grass amid the gravestones. The hot tears pricked her face as she lay there, exhausted from constantly flitting between happy and sad. She hated Harry for not being there when she needed him.

The wedding guests had waved off the bride and groom in their carriage, trotting off to their wedding reception at the local golf club where they would eat and drink too much. Aunty Jean would be in appropriate and Brian from the rugby club would no doubt pass out. Always the same. If Harry had been there, they would have stolen some cake and sat under a table somewhere, laughing at the dads trying to dance. But they had left Sarah in the grass. 'She'll be OK in a minute, you have to let her get it out of her system' they would be saying. 'it's all part of the process', 'she just needs time'.

Sarah's body eventually loosened. The tears dried and her breathing slowed down. She closed her eyes and felt the sun on her face. 'Where are you Harry?' she whispered. 'I need you'. She imagined his face, his eyes and his blond hair blowing in the breeze and the freckles on his sun kissed skin. They were so lucky living so close to the coast. But despite the lure of the vast bluey water and the soft yellow sand, they preferred to play up on the clifftop, up where they could see right across the bay, and the added advantage of avoiding the holiday makers and the noises that only appeared during the summer season. She felt the pinch of his fingers on her skin. She recalled her threatening him with a smack for pinching her. She saw him turn and run backwards, laughing and daring her to chase him. She called to him to come away from the edge, she begged him. She saw Harry's face the exact moment he lost his footing. She saw this body on the rocks below and she saw the light go from his eyes.

As the crowds began to form around his lifeless body, and sirens and screams floated up from the scene below, she saw Harry skip off into the distance, only turning back to smile at her, his dark lifeless eyes peeping through his floppy blonde hair. She knew he would never leave her and she lay on the cliff top,the sunshine on her face, and smiled.

2

The Delivery

She waits at the window. Her young face looks older than it should, her eyes dull and her skin pale. Her gaze is fixed on the gates at the end of the long sweeping driveway. She doesn't see the perfectly manicured gardens or the brightly coloured flowers that grow along the gravel path. They have tried to make it look attractive, they've used the garden to try to mask the heartache and sadness that lurks in the grand old house. For those who don't know, it's a lovely old house with a lovely garden. For those who do, it represents pain.

So she waited, her ears desperate to hear and not hear all at once. They would arrive soon. She had been told it would be today and that she should stay upstairs. A prisoner in her own life. She rested her head on the hard window pane and sighed, leaving a cloud of condensation on the glass. For a brief moment, she appreciated the coolness against her forehead, but it soon became hard and uncomfortable. But she wouldn't move. At 15, Mary felt that her world was about to come to an end. When that car arrived that would be it, it would all be over, and they would expect her to go home and carry on as normal. Normal. What did that mean?

She thought she had been a normal 14 year old, she had spent most of her Christmas holidays at her school friend Susan's house. She had met Susan during her first term at boarding school and very quickly realised that they came from opposite sides of the same town. Susan's parents worked all hours, and just like Mary's parents, they weren't around much. Susan's older brother, Joseph, had lots of friends who were always there too, making use of the empty house and the lack of authority. But that was nine months ago and, to her, it seemed like another world, another life. Now there were no more carefree afternoons in the park, no parties at houses where parents went out to work, no sneaking bottles of cheap beer from the larder, no stolen moments in the dark where no-one could see. A stolen moment in the dark had stolen her innocence and had catapulted her into a life where she didn't belong.

She glanced at the clock. Three minutes to go. Two o'clock they told her, like they were letting her know what time the shop shut or the number three bus was due. Just like that. And then, as if sensing her will for the clock to stop, they arrived.

The car pulled into the driveway slowly. She could see the lady in the front seat, all twinset and pearls and glowing. She hated and loved her instantly. Mary thought she looked nice. Kind. The man was older, he wore a too small suit and new brown shoes and looked more important than she suspected he was. They both hid their obvious excitement behind their formal clothes and shiny footwear. They walked hand in hand up to the front door and Mary heard a bell ring in the distance. Then silence. Mary's breath steamed up the window and she wiped it away angrily. She needed to see now more than ever. And she waited again. Waiting for them to come out. Waiting for one last look. Standing on a worn patch of carpet, her eyes were fixed on the driveway, her ears searching, desperate to hear one last sound.

It was edging toward the end of the summer and the air had a nip that warned of the impending autumn. The leaves were slowly turning, a summer of dancing leaving the flowers with no more energy. The nights would start drawing in soon. Her mother told her that would make things easier because she wouldn't be out so much, no one would see, no one would ask questions. It's for the best.

Mary wasn't sure what 'It's for the best' meant. Best for who? She wasn't able to go back to boarding school, they had already told her that. She had missed too much and, if truth be told, she had never been what they called a natural scholar. She wasn't old enough to keep the baby, that wasn't even an option for her, not that she was ever given the opportunity to even consider that decision. She wasn't old enough to be a mum, and wasn't young enough to save her childhood.

And then suddenly there they were. Mary heard polite laughter and muffled voices. Matron stood there, acting like God and the couple were smiling and nervous all at the same time. Mary wondered how someone could act so loving yet be so cruel, giving away a tiny life like a pound of apples. It's for the best. Mary never really understood that but she had been told it so many times that she thought it must be true. And damn the cooler weather. The bundle of blue blankets meant that she couldn't see properly. She reached up to the window, desperate for one last look, her fingers leaving smudges amongst the others that marked the glass. But he was handed over and in the car and gone in an instant. Gone. Matron glanced up at the window but Mary didn't see. Her gaze was fixed on the spot where the car had been.

She waited at the window. She didn't even know what she waited for any more. She had no choice but to wait. For something, anything. Waiting was all she had left, and so she waited by the window.

3

To Have And To Hold

She would quite often sit on the pub's stone wall, opposite the village church, and wait for the wedding party to come out. That was her favourite part of the weekend, when there was a wedding taking place. The church bells peeled out the signal and she would run from the garden to get a good spot. The other villagers who gathered there, pints in hand, used to laugh at her as she stretched up to get the best view. She loved the ceremony of it all, the ladies with their big hats, the men all smart and handsome in their finest and the children, in clothes so lovely that she didn't even know where you would go to buy them. The air was heavy with heady floral smells, no one ever quite sure if it exuded from the flowers or the heavily perfumed ladies. Sometimes there were horses, and if you got a nice carriage man, he would let you stroke them. But her most favourite bit of all was when they threw confetti, like petals, like snowflakes. She thought it was magical.

One day, that will be me, she thought. She had already planned what she would look like, she used to cut out pictures from magazines of dresses and flowers. She would often look at her mum's wedding picture. There was only one, tucked into the sleeve at the back of an album. Her mum wore a navy suit, and the man, who she assumed was her dad, had his hand on her shoulder. Her mum held a small bouquet of flowers over her protruding waist.

She traced her finger over the couple and thought about how sad it was that her mum didn't get to wear a big white dress. She would never *have* to get married, when she got married it would be because they were in love. So in love that they glowed. Their wedding photo would be above the fireplace so that everyone could see, not hidden away at the back of an album.

Amy's mum never married again. She had more children but she never glowed and never got married. Amy quite often still heard the church bells at the weekend, but by the time she had rounded up all her siblings, she often missed the bridal party exit. She still dreamed of her dress though; she still dreamed of what her husband would be like. Handsome, intelligent, well dressed. Her mum would laugh at her and tell her to get real. Men like that don't exist, and when they do they're only around until they get what they want. Amy never really understood that. Surely she would be what they wanted? Surely the only thing that any man wanted was a wife who loved him. She could do that. She knew how to love. She had brothers and sisters and a mum and she loved them. And they loved her. Her mum often told her just how much when she was too hungover to cook tea or when the ironing needed doing. Her brothers and sisters told her all the time when they wanted to go to the park or were hungry. When she got married she would be loved and she would love them.

Simple.

Her friends at school had boyfriends, but Amy could never quite pinpoint what it was the boys wanted. She didn't wear the right skirt or her hair wasn't quite the right colour. They're just boys she told herself. Men notice the important things. Her Maths teacher, Steven, noticed her. He noticed when she had her hair different or when she wore a new skirt.

He had taught her lots of things, both in and out of the classroom. She didn't need boys when she could get so much more from men and they told her she was special, that she was worth more, that she was beautiful. This is what love is like she thought, this is the sort of glow that brides get. If only circumstances were different. If only she were older or he were younger. If only he wasn't her teacher. All these things were stopping her from getting her wedding picture. He wanted to be with her, she could tell, he just couldn't. She understood that. She accepted that. She knew that he would if he could, he told her that he would if he could, but teachers are so busy in the evenings with marking and parents' evenings and stuff.

She had been so excited when she left school. She knew that now there was nothing stopping them from being together. She counted the days until he was back at work in September so she could contact him. Then they could make plans, plan a future.

She flicked through the local paper, circling office junior jobs and bar work. She would earn some money over the summer and surprise him. They could get a flat, she could help with the bills. She had already seen the most amazing duvet cover with pink hearts and matching curtains.

She hadn't spent as much time revising as she could have and so she wasn't expecting the best exam results, but she had spent lots of time with him when he wasn't busy with his own work and stuff. He'd sometimes call at the last minute and she had dropped everything to meet him. She just didn't have the time to study, what with looking after her siblings and her mum and everything else. But it didn't matter, she would get a job, something, anything, just to help out.

She sat at the kitchen table, enjoying a rare moment's piece as her siblings played in the garden. Her eyes scanned down the announcements section. She liked to look at the birthdays, read the messages to loved ones, and look at the funny photos. Her eyes were drawn to the wedding announcements, she could never resist a wedding photo. Amy traced the outline of the dress with her finger, it wasn't something she would have chosen, it was too plain for Amy. The flowers looked pretty though, although she could only see them in the grainy black and white newspaper print. She could tell from the giveaway archway setting of the photo that it was a traditional church wedding. She approved of that.

Her eyes scanned over the groom. Amy was a little taken back by the side profile of the suited gentleman who was holding his new wife's hand and looking at her as if she was the most beautiful woman in the world. She picked up the newspaper and looked more closely at the picture. No. No, it couldn't be. In a moment of panic her eyes darted to the bottom of the photo as she desperately attempted to read the text, her eyes looking for one name in particular.

And then she saw it. She put her hand to her mouth. She thought she was going to be sick. She panicked and reread it just in case she had made a mistake. But no, the new Mr & Mrs Steven Shaw would like to thank everyone for their kind gifts on the occasion of their wedding. She sat, numb, staring out of the window, her heart pounding. How has this happened? He never mentioned a girlfriend. Never. He lived with his sick parents, that's why she could never go to his house. He was busy looking after them. He never ever mentioned a girl, she was sure of it. He had told her he wanted her. He had told her that they would be together after the summer. But the summer was nearly over and she had not heard from him. Neither did she hear from him in September, or ever again.

Amy called the school one day and pretended to be a parent, but apparently, he had left the school at the end of the academic year and they were not at liberty to tell her where. And that was that. No apology, no explanation. She was left with nothing but a bar job and an empty heart.

Amy had managed to get a job in the local Spar shop at the end of the summer when her siblings had all gone back to school. She liked keeping busy and the extra money came in handy. It gave her something to leave the house for. As soon as she was old enough, she also got a bar job a couple of evenings a week. Stan, the landlord, had always had a soft spot for Amy, he remembered her as a young girl balancing herself on the stone wall outside on a Saturday afternoon. He knew the family, Amy's mum was well known in there, for a few reasons, none of them particularly complimentary.

Chris used to come into the bar straight from work, still wearing his suit, tie loosened from around his neck and jacket thrown over the back of his chair. He'd always insist she changed the music when he got there - he wasn't a Spice Girls fan. He was different, not like that liar from school. He made Amy laugh and she was drawn to his generosity; he always bought her a drink, or slipped her a tip. She was impressed with his smart suit and mobile phone, she didn't know many people with a mobile phone. She used to laugh at the way he always patted his pocket to see if his phone was still there. And he was honest with her. She knew he was married, but it wasn't a proper marriage. She knew that he lived with her in a big house, she knew that the four bedrooms were once occupied by a family of five, but now, all grown up, it left two empty bedrooms and two occupied. He said that his wife had been a miserable bitch for years and the sex had never been great. He was sick of hearing about hot flushes and headaches. He was sick of hearing about her fucking job, she thought she was so important driving around in her flash car in her designer heels. Bitch. She had never shown any interest in him or his work and he was a man for fuck's sake; he had needs. And so he would tell her all about how unhappy he was, and how he needed to be with someone like her instead, someone happy. Someone attractive. Someone special.

It had all started when he had been in the bar one Friday evening. He told her we wanted to take her out somewhere special, to treat her like a princess. That was enough for Amy. No one had ever wanted to do nice things for her. The eldest of 4, she was the go-to girl for chores and shopping and cleaning, not for being spoilt. And so it began. Their first date was their first time. He told her he loved her and she believed him. He made time for her, when he wasn't busy with work. He took her to places in other towns to treat her. He even bought her a special phone to contact him on – so he wouldn't get his work calls mixed up. She was so lucky. Yes he was still married, but she didn't care. It wasn't a real marriage. He didn't glow.

After yet another hour or two on the back seat of his car, Amy had decided that she wanted to talk to him, discuss the future. She wanted to know when he was going to tell his wife he was leaving her. He had promised for months that he would do it soon, and although she would never tell him what to do, she also wanted to know where she stood.

The novelty of finishing work and meeting him in his car was starting to wear off. The hotel rooms weren't so frequent now, he told her he was saving for a divorce. But then he would appear in a new car, or with a new phone, or watch. He would get angry if she mentioned it, the same way he would get angry if her shifts changed, or if she phoned when she wasn't supposed to. But it was because he was stressed with work and living with that woman she told herself, not because of her. She was starting to get fed up with the lack of commitment. She wanted to plan holidays, to plan a future, she just wanted him to commit. He was always so busy and now it was always just a quick drink and a quick one in the car. She needed more from him. She needed him to be with her, to move in together, to get married. That couldn't happen while he was still with his wife.

She decided to play hard to get. She had never done that before.

So the next time he would call, she had decided that she would tell him she was busy. Or not answer. Or tell him not unless he had left his wife. She just had to be strong and not give in to him again.

The red lights made her face glow the way it does when you spend an hour too long in the sunshine. All she could see ahead of her were red lights. 'It's a sign' she thought to herself. 'This is a sign telling me that I shouldn't be doing this'. She debated getting off the bus and walking home, but she was already more than halfway there. And she had spent so long getting ready. And she was wearing new underwear. What is the point of wearing new underwear if no one is going to see it? The next time she wore it, it wouldn't be new. So no, she would just sit on the bus in the traffic and get there whenever she got there. She turned up the volume on her Walkman to try to drown her thoughts.

As her head nodded in time to the Backstreet Boys, she glanced out of the window. Across the road, she could see straight through the window of a Pizza Hut. Sat in the window was a middle aged couple. They were laughing over something, something one of them had said. She smiled to herself. That's nice, she thought. She looked again. The lady looked like she was telling a story. The man was looking at her. Not just looking at her, but seeing her. And then she felt a knot in her stomach. They're in love. They are in the kind of love that you wish for, they glowed. She sighed. She would get off the bus as soon as she could. New underwear or not, some things just weren't worth it.

The glow of red gradually faded and, one by one, the traffic started to move. She panicked. She wanted to get off but she couldn't. She wanted someone to see her the way that man in Pizza Hut had looked at that woman. She wanted someone. She wanted him. So she turned her music down so she could concentrate. She wanted to say the exact right thing to him this evening. Their last meeting had ended in another row - she'd wanted to talk, she wanted to know where she stood, but he said that time was precious and they couldn't waste it. So they didn't talk and she didn't get any answers, and that night she cried herself to sleep again. But tonight he had contacted her and told her that he had made sure that he was free all night. He wanted to spend it with her. Just her. And she was excited.

She stepped off the bus at the stop across from the hotel and checked her make-up in her compact mirror. She let out a sigh. She looked good. She knew that she did. If he didn't commit to her now, when she looked like this, then there was no hope at all. This was as good as it got. And as she looked across the road, there he was, waiting for her. She smiled. He's so romantic, she thought. She crossed over the road and walked over to him. He pulled her into the foyer and kissed her urgently before reaching for her hand. She looked down, and her heart sank. She wouldn't get any answers tonight. He was still wearing the ring.

4

Down The Aisles

I watch him as he stands staring at the shelf in front of him. I first noticed him in the bakery aisle and thought he looked quite handsome, and they do say don't they, that a supermarket is a good place to meet someone. Although *they*, the people I know who say that, are not actually single, so I'm not entirely sure where they have that fact from. But nevertheless, I need to eat so if it happens whilst I'm stocking up the cupboards then I'll take that as a bonus. Not only am I running out of baked beans, I am also running out of dating options. Everyone I know now either has a partner, a husband, some even have children. I'm going to get left on the shelf if I don't get fixed up soon.

I bet he has a wife at home though, the handsome ones usually do, a really beautiful wife who leaves the house in the morning without looking in the mirror first. I bet she is great with children and knows how to make meals without a cookbook. He puts something in his basket; I know it's a tin of soup because I've just put one in myself. It is the only thing in his basket so I expect he will be in here for a while yet. I look at his finger, just to check. No ring! This is promising, a tin of soup and no wedding ring. He's on the move, down the pasta aisle. I've never really understood why there are so many different shapes of pasta. Bows, shells, twisty ones, round spaghetti, flat spaghetti; I bet there are people in the world who know exactly what type to use for what meal. I just get whatever is on offer. I don't even like pasta all that much if I'm honest. He doesn't put in any pasta, only some of that microwavable rice. I think he must be single.

He must have come straight from work. He has a lovely purple coloured tie on and his shoes are ever so shiny. I look down at mine and wish I had given mine a clean this morning. Actually, I wish I had made a bit more of an effort today. In future I am going to do my hair in the morning and make sure I have some lipstick in my bag for occasions like this. I'm sure I look like a mess. I'll keep my hair over my face a bit so he can't see what I look like. I don't want to scare him off just yet; we haven't gone down the freezer aisle yet.

That's it, definitely single. 5 for £4 microwave meals for one. I wonder why he hasn't chosen the expensive ones? Maybe he has children...maybe he has an ex-wife and a huge maintenance bill. His suit is too smart for him to have a crap job. Mind you, I don't have an ex or kids or a crap job and I buy them. Oh. He's gone for the tomato pasta one. I hate that one. Oh God I hope he wouldn't make that on a first dinner date.

This is new territory for me, the wine aisle. I don't normally buy wine. I wish I could drink it, women with a wine glass always look so sophisticated. I might buy a bottle to make him think I'm one of those women. What sort? Is there a sort? Oh God there are so many. He's picked up a bottle of red. It's Argentinian. (I know this because the sign at the top of the shelf tells me). I thought wine came from France? I'm going in, I'm going to get one. We will catch each other's eye in a minute and have a moment – then later we will share our wine together. Now which one....

Shit, he's gone.

Ah, I can see him at the till. I'm going to go behind him. I'll make a really funny comment about what he has in his basket. Then he'll ask me over for tea and I'll tell him only if I don't get the tomato pasta one. He'll laugh and think I'm charming.

Damn, I'm too late. Now I'm stuck behind a grey haired lady who smells of cats and meat pie.

The checkout lady looks miserable today. Again. She doesn't even ask me if I want any help with my packing. Mind you, there's not much to pack, I've not really been paying attention. The lady scans the tin of soup.

I look at my tin of soup and no wedding ring.

sigh

5

Maybe

When Sally was 12 years old she saw her first dead body. When she was 13 she went to her first funeral and when she was 14 she was so afraid of death that she tried to avoid people over the age of 60. She would avoid watching the news and would turn down the radio on the hour – she didn't want to hear about death, dying, the dead or the unwell. In fact, Sally was so afraid of dying that she had often contemplated taking her own life just to get it out of the way.

At the age of 19, she wished she was dead. She looked at the other girls she knew, all lip gloss and hair dye. How did they manage to get through the day and still smile? She hated them, she hated the way they smiled at everything, how they laughed, how they blushed when young men winked at them. They never winked at her. They crossed the road when they saw her. And Sally would be relieved. She didn't want them to look at her. To see her.

She used to like people, she used to be a chatty little girl before it happened. She sometimes went to her friend's house for tea. She loved that, she loved it when they all sat around a table talking about their days. Sometimes there would just be a mum, or a dad, but often there was both. They asked her questions and listened to her answers. She loved that.

She'd never invite them to come to her house. They didn't need to see that, what with her mum sat smoking one fag after another and forgetting she had a child to feed. Adding another child in the mix could possibly tip her over the edge. It wasn't a child around for tea that tipped her over the edge in the end. Sally didn't actually know what it was. She knew that her mother had told her to hurry up and get to school that morning, she remembered her shouting after her 'get your fucking ugly face out of my house'. And when she got home, her mum was asleep. So fast asleep that she never woke up again.

Sally's hooded jacket hid her face and just in case anyone saw past that, her eyes were so covered in black eyeliner they were hardly recognisable. She hated herself. She hated how she looked and she hated the way people looked at her. They didn't know what to say to her and she had nothing to say to them.

Sally had feared death nearly all her life. She had feared she would take her own life. She had hoped someone else would save her the trouble. When Sally was 20 that very nearly happened. She trusted a man who hurt her. Really hurt her. And after she feared him so much that she let him get away with it.

At 23, just three years later, Sally felt that maybe, just maybe she could face the world again. The hood had gone and the eyeliner, although not completely gone, allowed her pretty almond shaped eyes to be seen. She made sure she kept her wrists covered and now and again, she smiled, although only at women. People no longer crossed over the road when they saw her, and as each day went by, she thought more about living than dying. She did normal things, she went to work, she went to the supermarket, she even went to the pub once. She went to the opticians when she was supposed to, and she went to the dentist when it was time. One thing she didn't do though was go to the doctors. She should have gone to the doctors. They would have told her that they had caught it in time, that they could do something. But she didn't because she was afraid. Afraid of dying.

6

The Office

It was his name on the business card; in hard edged font, deep black ink on crisp, hard white card, the company logo in the corner reminding him of who owned him. He had a stash of them in the glove compartment of his car. He also had quite a few of them in his kitchen bin. Every so often he called the office to order more, then he'd keep half and throw half away. It made him seem popular. Liked. All the things he thought that he wasn't.

It didn't come naturally to him, all this schmoozing, the net-working, the dinners, the events. He was quite at home in his local with a pint, not in some chrome and glass bar sipping mojitos and cosmopolitans. He *did* wear a designer suit, but because it fitted well, not because of the name of the label. He didn't care who or what Prada was. His watch wasn't the size of a satellite dish and his car, although very smart and shiny, did what he wanted it to do, got him from A to B. Yet still his boss insisted that he play the game, create this impression, impress. He knew how to impress. His in-depth knowledge and his natural ability with figures impressed everyone he met. Why would slapping on a designer label and a few diamantés help?

He rearranged the jar of perfectly sharpened pencils on his desk and closed his shiny state of the art laptop. His email pinged just before it clicked shut. He sighed, and wondered how he had gotten here, how it had come to this. A slave to the system.

He ran his soft manicured fingers through his dark hair and sat for a moment with his head in his hands. At the age of 34 he thought he would be stepping away from the pressure of work. He dreamed of leaving the office at 5pm and travelling back home, imagining his loving wife waiting for him at the door with a smile and a kiss. They would cook dinner together in their open plan kitchen, the aroma filling the house with comfort and warmth. His children, all three of them, would come bounding down the stairs, all dressed beautifully with his wife's blond hair and his piercing blue eyes. He would shower them with kisses before telling them to go and wash their hands ready for dinner. Then they would all sit around the huge wooden table and would create a hum of chatter about their days and their dreams.

The vibration of his mobile phone startled him back to reality. It was her. Why wouldn't she leave him alone? He had submitted the proposal hours ago, well before the deadline, what could she possibly want from him now? He watched the phone ring and then fall silent. He breathed with relief. He sat for a moment with his eyes closed, willing not to hear the notification of an answerphone message. Nothing. He picked up his briefcase and headed out to the car park. His phone vibrated again just as he was opening the car door. He didn't check to see who it was this time. It was 15.15, Sarah always called at 15.15 without fail. She would give him an update and to see what time he would be arriving for his visit.

'Hi Sarah, I'm just getting into the car'
   'Paul? Is that you? Is everything OK?'
   Shit. It wasn't his Sarah at all. It was her.
   'Ah Dana. Sorry. I thought you were someone else, I'm just leaving the office'
   'Really Paul, as if you could get me mixed up with another woman, but seriously, I could do with a quick chat about the proposal. Can you call into my office on your way home?' Paul panicked. He really didn't want to go there, she would be alone and it was Friday, she would try to get him to go with her to the bar. He just wanted to get to the home. Things hadn't been going well this week and he was concerned.

   'Now Dana? Only I need to get back home, I have plans this evening'. He had managed to create a persona of himself at work as a family man, a man who had a successful wife and super intelligent children who either played a musical instrument or excelled at some form of sport. He liked to keep his personal life personal. If only they knew. If only they knew that the only thing he had going on outside of work was caring for his sick mother. There were no siblings to take the strain, just him. It had always just been the two of them, he wouldn't let her down. The care home was the best in the county and it came with an extortionate price tag - he owed her that comfort at least, especially if he couldn't always be with her.

   'Yes, I won't keep you long. This won't wait until after the weekend Paul and I have a lot of money resting on this proposal.

If this is successful it could mean a lot more work for you and your company'.

Paul was already heading to her office. He knew she wouldn't take no for an answer and the sooner he got there the sooner he could leave. He always tried to visit the home on a Friday to visit his mum, but then he often cancelled too. But today he needed to see her. His mum thought he was ever so successful with his big firm in the city. She actually had no idea what he did but he had a nice big shiny car and wore a suit so that was good enough for her. And he was busy. All the time. But he sent her flowers so she knew he loved her.

Paul pulled up outside the imposing glass building that Dana reigned over. Her office was on the top floor. Clad in black and chrome furniture with rugs on the floor. Paul often thought it looked more like a living room than an office. Maybe that was the point. She spent so much of her time there that Paul sometimes wondered if she ever went home, or if home even existed.

Dana was such a prominent figure in the city, uber successful and powerful. She had brought companies to their knees and had MDs wrapped around her little finger. But her interest in Paul was something else. He excited her with his intelligence and ideas. She saw him as a shining light in a bleak economy and she wanted him. She wanted him in her company. She had tried previously to get him out of the office environment, to show him all of the good things that he could achieve , the glitz, the glamour, the countless parties and women. But he was hard. He wouldn't budge. He was loyal to his firm and she respected that.

What was wrong with the man? If she could just get him to thaw a little. Just a little.

Paul got into the lift and pressed the button that would take him to the 15th floor. He took out his phone to check his messages. Nothing. He wondered why he hadn't received a call from the home yet. He really needed to get this meeting done with and get off to visit his mum. The lift came to a stop. The doors opened and he stepped out into the shiny corridor. He paused for a moment to make a call. He would let his mum know that he was definitely going to be there tonight, as soon as he possibly could. He dialled the number and waited.

'Hello? Sarah?'

Sarah sounded harassed.

'Paul, is that you?'

'How is she today Sarah? I couldn't get away from the office, but I'll be setting off in about an hour'

'Paul, wait...'

'I'll be there for 8pm Sarah, can you just tell her to hold on until then? I've been so busy today and I've just got one more meeting and...'

'Paul, please, just let me speak for a minute. It's too late Paul, she's gone.'

7

Ex

Nadia put down the pieces of paper on the desk and sighed. Why did he always ask her to read his work? 'Be honest' he had said. She suspected he didn't really mean that, because if she were to tell him that it was the most boring, uninspiring piece of drivel she had ever had the misfortune to read then he may be a little upset. So she thought about something constructive to say. How about changing that first sentence, how about adding something funny, how about scrap the whole thing and start again.

She left the table and put the kettle on. The hum and hissing of the water reminded her of the time that he had tried to make her coffee in one of those silver things you put on the stove. It had all gone horribly wrong; they had sat in the stench of burnt coffee and air freshener. They had laughed about it then. Now she just thought he was a prat.

Nadia dunked the teabag in and out of the cup. He hated it when she did that. 'you're making a mess' he would say and followed her around with the cloth wiping the surfaces like he was trying to eliminate third world debt. 'It's just tea – leave it' she would say, but he would drone on about how once you start leaving it then it would stain and then they'd have to replace the work surfaces and he wasn't made of money you know.

She sat back down. They laughed a lot at first. She once dropped a jar of pickled onions on the kitchen floor; they had played marbles with them before cleaning up. He had once dropped a whole bottle of bubble bath in the bathroom, the clean-up operation resembled an Ibiza foam party. They had spent most of their time laughing then. But now he only saw how it had stained the grouting; and he'd stopped buying her bubble bath long ago. No, she was glad to be out of that.

It had been fun, she thought it might have gone further, but they had decided to just stay friends, because that's what you did when you were an adult apparently – although to be honest, she would quite gladly have walked away and never seen him again. 'Moody little prat' she thought.

She picked up the sheets of paper again. Why on earth had he asked her to read this? She couldn't have been less interested if she had tried, and it's not like she would ever hear him read it anyway. She considered telling him she was too busy, but then he would think she was being a stroppy cow. If she read it and didn't comment he would think she was being awkward, that she wasn't pleased for them. No, she had to make some comments. So she took out her pen and circled a couple of words. *Perhaps change 'pleasure' to 'honour', she thought, 'and perhaps change 'beautiful' to 'enchanting'.* Changing for changing sake.

33

Who cares? Take out the whole paragraph for all I care. Take out 'thank you for coming', take out 'cannot wait to spend my life with her', just erase the whole bloody lot. Stupid little prat. It will never last anyway, not when he starts moaning about what she is wearing, or the way she chews, or the sound she makes when she breathes.

She picked up the papers and threw them in the recycling. No, fuck it, he can write it himself, and she made another cup of tea, and didn't wipe up the mess.

8

Visiting Hour

I sit and watch you. The walls in here are gleaming despite their tired appearance and the smell of disinfectant is so strong that despite only being here for 45 minutes, I struggle to recall what fresh air smells like. The wallpaper is a subtle pale yellow, a floral design which I imagine used to be quite a statement 20 years ago. There are some yellow flowers in the blue vase on the windowsill. They are bright and happy, casting a yellow glow on the white paint. I don't know how long they have been there or where they have come from but they make me smile. A bit of life. Yellow like the sunshine. Like buttercups. Like lemons. I'd love to see a lemon right now, cut up in a glass with some ice and something strong. I'll make do with the not quite strong enough tea.

I probably should have bought you flowers, but it just seems like a waste of money. You didn't really like flowers when you weren't in here. You used to moan when I bought them, say that you hadn't got the right shaped vase and you'd have to keep changing the water. You seemed to change your mind about which flowers you hated the most every time I bought them. That's why I stopped. So it seems silly to start again now.

I'll be honest with you, I am a bit bored. You haven't woken up in all the time I have been sitting here, which feels about 5 years. It has only been 45 minutes. 45 long, slow minutes. I count to 60 to see how long a minute was but got bored. I glance around the room to see what everyone else is doing. The family on my left are looking at some photographs. The old man they surround is sitting in a burgundy leather-look chair nodding and smiling. He quite clearly has no idea what is going on. I'm not even convinced he knows who these people are. At least he is awake.

I've already been to the vending machine once this visit. I bought a Snickers. I've been trying to get a bit of peanut from between my teeth ever since. One bonus of you being asleep is that you can't make your usual comment about if I should be eating it and reminding me of how easily I put on weight. I have actually lost a bit of weight over the last few months. Not that you would ever comment on it. And I've given up telling you because you never acknowledge it, only tell me how much more weight you've lost than me. To be fair, you'd win hands down at the moment.

I look at you. You don't look ill, you just look like you are asleep. Like you are every time I come. I wonder if you do it on purpose. I wonder if you are actually awake, also counting down the minutes until I go home. I get up to leave, feeling that I should really bend over and give you a kiss. I don't. See you next week you miserable cow. And I go home and the guilt hits me. Every time. Every single time.

9

Ever the Optimist

She looked at the clock. 11.15pm. It was too late now, even if he asked her to go now, it was too late. She looked at herself in the mirror. She had made an effort, she looked nice, not too nice, not like she was trying too hard, but she looked pretty. What waste she thought. No-one had seen her face this evening, no-one would see her face except her. Why was it that no one saw her when she thought she looked nice. They saw the everyday, busy, stressed, hurried face, but no-one saw the one at night, the one that longed to be loved, to be seen.

She checked the clock again. 11.27. She'd give him until 11.30, no, 11.45. He had until then to say the word. She would go running. He had her waiting on three words, three words she often heard from him late at night. Not quite the three words she wanted, but they came close enough. Just one text, please, just tell me that you want me. She lay on the bed, fully clothed, willing her phone to illuminate. She checked she still had a signal. Of course she had. There was no message.

When it got to midnight she gave up. She took off her new underwear and folded up her clothes neatly and climbed into bed. She wouldn't take off her make up just yet, just in case. She placed her phone next to her and closed her eyes. She imagined him lay on his bed, thinking about her, phone in hand, fingers hovering over the screen. She almost ached to hear from him. But she had no control. He held the cards and only let her play on his terms. But that didn't stop her from dreaming of what it could be like, if he just let her in for more than a few hours on a Saturday night. If he just spent some time with her so they could talk, get to know one another properly. Not just a quick rendezvous now and again when he needed a lift home from the pub. She was sure that he would realise how much he wanted her, more than like this. So she lay on the bed, makeup still on, phone still on, waiting.

She opened her eyes in a panic. What time was it? She had fallen asleep! She reached for her phone and unlocked the screen. 1.20am. Nothing. No message. No missed call. She opened up her Facebook to see if she could see where he had been, where he was. Nothing. She sighed. Her heart sinking and her hopes fading. It wouldn't happen tonight now. Not this week. So she lay back down, phone still on, make up still on, and closed her eyes, in her head, making up her own ending.

One day, she thought, one day I'll get those three words again. 'I want you'. And she would go running. Without question, to just spend an hour in his company. If I just got one more hour with him he'll realise.

She drifted off to sleep.

The next morning she woke up, checked her phone, wiped off her makeup and got dressed. Maybe next weekend. Yes, next weekend he'll want me.

10

The Dating Game

'That's it', she said. That . Is. It. I am NEVER going on a blind date EVER AGAIN. EVER. 'You're always saying that' laughed Anna. Anna and Sarah had been best of friends for years. Not the lifelong school friend 'I know everything about you' type friend, but more like the 'I know enough about you to know that I like you;' kind of friend. They had met when Sarah had started a new job in a café, she just worked a few hours to subsidise her shopping habit and put petrol in her car whilst she was at college. Anna was full time and had been there since she left school and Sarah knew she liked her the minute she heard her call a customer a 'nobber' under her breath. Anyone who had the word 'nobber' in their vocabulary shot straight up the scale in Sarah's estimation. They both loved cake, they both loved cheesy pop music and they both had the same loathing for men who adjusted themselves in public.

The blind date had all been Anna's idea. "It will be fun," she had said. 'For who?' replied Sarah with genuine confusion. It's not like she hadn't been on a blind date before. She had once met a lovely man who had bought her an orange juice and a bag of cheese and onion crisps. They exchanged pleasantries and he had proceeded to tell her all about the ex-girlfriend who had left him for a croissant twister and the bakery where they both worked. It hadn't ended well apparently, escalating to a nasty brawl by the cherry topping machine. Sarah never saw him again and made a mental note to permanently remove cherry bakewells from her weekly shop.

Then the man with the sports car. He wasn't too bad. He had promised to take her away for the weekend after half an hour of meeting. 'We'll go somewhere posh, somewhere classy yea babe?' Sarah had agreed, I mean come on, he had a sports car! He dressed well and he wore nice shoes. It went downhill though. Quickly. Yes he did drive a sports car. His mummy let him have it at the weekend now and again. During the date he had told her how he was going to take her to that lovely place where that girl who wrote that famous diary came from. Sarah would be the first to confess that she wasn't what you would call 'bookish', but she did know who Anne Frank was and was quite excited at the thought of a trip along a canal and pictured herself frolicking through the tulips. Turns out that sports car man wasn't 'bookish' either. Or anything else for that matter. And Anne Frank did most definitely NOT come from Tywyn. It would never work out, sports car or not. And so Sarah had stopped blind-dating for a while.

'One day I'll meet a man who makes me feel excited inside. Not the sort of excited you get at Christmas, but the sort of excitement that makes you feel that you can fly'. And she desperately wanted to fly. She wanted to wake up in the morning knowing that there was someone in the world who was thinking about her. She wanted to be the first thought on someone's mind. She wanted someone to change their plans for her, not fit her in around them. And she was prepared to wait. That sort of person was worth waiting for.

Anna was a little more cynical. She had been with Simon for years and although Sarah was in no doubt that they loved each other, it didn't seem to be in a flying excitement kind of way. But they seemed happy, if not perhaps a little bored, but happy nonetheless.

'You won't find a man like that by sitting at home watching Love Island' Anna warned; 'you need to get out there!' Sarah knew this. She knew she had to get out there – but where was there? She knew where it wasn't, she knew in her local town the closest she would get to that flying feeling would be down the high street to escape the locals who thought their luck was in. So she had attempted online dating. And it had seemed fun at first, she had chatted to some lovely men, and despite the 2 she had plucked up the courage to meet, she was sure that Mr Right was just around the corner, or profile, or whatever. And so then she found Liam. Ahhhh Liam. On paper he ticked all of the boxes. She was cautious this time and asked all the right questions. He had a sound knowledge of music, he knew who Anne Frank was and where she lived. He had his own car – she hadn't asked how it was paid for as she thought that was a bit crass, but it wasn't his mothers and that was enough for Sarah. She had done the necessary stalking on social media and all of his answers seemed to add up with her findings. So she agreed to meet him.

She pulled onto the car park and parked far enough away to be inconspicuous but with a viewpoint of the doorway so she could assess the situation. She also had a clear exit in case she decided to back out. Then she waited. She was an hour early – but she didn't want him to see her arrive because then he would know she was there. She checked her face in the rear view mirror, she sprayed more perfume and she looked at his picture online again just so that she knew what she was looking for. In her head this one had more potential than the others. He had said all the right things to her, he made her feel excited when she logged on and saw a message from him. She had even stopped chatting to the other men so that she could concentrate on him. She liked the idea of him and her together. The vibration of the phone in her hand made her jump. It was a text from Anna.

Well?

He's not here yet. Waiting on car park.

What r u wearing?

Black jeans, red top – the 1 that makes my boobs look perky

Gud choice. Txt me when ur in the pub'

K

Gd luck. B careful x

Xxx

She put her phone in her bag. 19.27. They had arranged to meet at 19.30. She prayed he wouldn't be late. That would untick one of her boxes. She hated people being late. She also cursed herself for not giving him her phone number. She wanted to appear a little coy and hard to get, but now she had no way of knowing if he was there or not. There was no one outside, but then she had not really been paying attention whilst she was texting Anna. So she took a deep breath and got out of the car.

She walked across the car park making sure she looked confident and sexy just in case he was in his car waiting for her. But no-one appeared. She entered the pub and looked around the room desperately hoping to see a familiar face. And there he was. He stood up to greet her and her heart immediately sank. 5'6 he had said. She had instantly knocked an inch off because that's what people do, she was always 5 '5 on paper, but the reality was more 5' 4. So she was expecting 5'5...not 5'2. She glanced at his feet, half expecting to see school shoes. His shoes were OK, very small size, but OK. She didn't know whether to laugh or cry. Why did people do that? She wouldn't have minded 5'2 if she'd have been expecting 5'2. It's not like he could have hidden the fact! The fact that he had lied immediately raised a red flag that this was a man with self esteem issues. *OK Emma, calm down. You can do this, stop overthinking.* She smiled and said hi and he ushered her toward the bar. She politely ordered a diet coke and they sat down. *Deep breath, here we go.*

She nodded and smiled politely whilst in her head calculating when would be an appropriate moment to leave. She heard all about his previous relationships. All about Jackie who had a boob job, all about Sharon who turned out to be gay. All about them. All. About. Them. She knew more about his life in the space of half an hour than she needed to know, and she doubted that if asked, he wouldn't even be able to recall what she did for a job. It wasn't what you would call a two way conversation. She let her mind drift off to an alternative life, where she would now be sat across from a man who thought she was enchanting, beautiful, special. Not some incessant talker with a string of failed relationships and an annoying habit of humming to himself during the awkward pauses. She excused herself and went to the toilet. She wished she could have the courage to just tell him that it wasn't going to work out, that she was pleased to meet him but she'd quite like to go home now. But she couldn't. She wasn't confident in that respect, she didn't want to hurt his feelings. So she sat on the toilet and texted Anna...

☹

Oh no!

Awful. He is 2ft tall and hums.

What? Hums as in smells???

No. actually hums. Hmmmmmm. All. The.Time

Go home!

How?

Tell him you're constipated. Or have thrush. Anything

I can't. Help.

Shall I come and rescue u?

No. I'll make excuses in a min. txt u l8r.x

Xxxx

She did wonder how long you could stay in the toilet for before someone got the hint and went home. She had already been there for about 20 minutes. Perhaps he would just have gone. As she pushed open the door to re-enter the bar she breathed a sigh of relief. The table where they had sat was now occupied by two old men drinking pints and sharing a bag of pork scratchings. *Phew. Lucky escape.*

She felt quite empowered inside and almost skipped toward the exit. And then she heard it. All across the room. 'Saaraahh', all singsongy. She froze. Oh god. He hadn't left at all, just moved over to the sofas, to the comfy area, where all the couples were sitting all cosy and close. *Shit*, she needed to think quickly. She was so close to the door she could almost taste freedom, but no, her feet started to turn around and before she knew it she was sitting next to him, smack in the middle of coupledom. Gross. He had already bought her another drink. She was trapped. For at least long enough for her to drink half a pint of coke.

He didn't stop talking, where was all of this information coming from? She didn't need to know where he had his first holiday, his first foreign food, his first sexual encounter. She wasn't even listening any more. She just wanted to go home. She consoled herself by the fact that the pub would have to close at some point. They would have to leave at some point. They couldn't stay here all night. 'It's *our* pub now, our special place' she heard him say. 'How lovely' she responded. 'What an ick' she thought.

When the ice melts in my glass I'm going to tell him I need to go, she said to herself, feeling a little comforted by the fact she had a plan. She held the glass in her hands just to help it along a little. If only she were more assertive, if only she had just been honest. She had had such high hopes and it had all gone wrong so very quickly. She was always doing this, sticking in situations because she didn't have the balls to be assertive. It made her sad. She felt that she constantly lived her life doing what other people wanted her to do. He's going to try and kiss me soon, she thought, and I am going to have to kiss him back. She prayed he didn't want to do anything else. She just wanted to go home. She didn't want to be groped in the back of a car. The ice had

46

melted, she took a deep breath.

'I've had a really lovely evening'

'Me too.'

'But I really have to go now.'

'OK I'll walk you to your car.'

Wow. That was easy. Why hadn't I just done that sooner, like 2 hours ago? She put her coat on and he held the door open for her. *Well that wasn't so bad. I mean, in the grand scheme of things that was OK.* They walked to the car, in time to his humming. She fumbled in her bag for her keys and then it happened. He called her name and she looked up at him and she knew this was the moment, this was the moment that he had decided they were going to share their first kiss. She debated for a second whether to just get in the car, but she didn't want to seem rude. And actually, it hadn't been that bad of an evening. She needed to deal with this one carefully. She didn't want to annoy him. Maybe she should just close her eyes and get it over with. She must have debated this long enough for him to realise that the kiss wasn't going to happen. She expected him to protest, but to her surprise smiled at her, quite sweetly.

So, can I have your number then?

Shit don't ruin this now Sarah, you can get away and delete his profile and never hear from him again. Do not give him your number!

She looked at him convincingly, 'Not until the second date'

'Ah I see —we're playing that game are we! Well I am going to message you the minute I get home and we can arrange something'

'Brilliant. I will log on as soon as I get in.'

She got into the car and shut the door and drove off all in one movement. Left him there standing in the car park. She was brave now; now she laughed. As if there was going to be a second date.

11

The Perfume

It was a gift, a beautifully presented, beautifully packaged gift in a box made of expensive red cardboard and a silver bow that glittered in the light. A reward for the turning of age. She had craved this since she browsed the testers in the department store in town. She would walk around waving the thin paper strips with a variety of scents, but this one, she had sprayed on her wrist. This one was special. For the rest of the day, she couldn't stop herself from continually breathing in the scent at every opportunity, raising her wrist to her nose whenever she needed a reminder of the heady floral scent that made her feel glamorous, beautiful and confident, all the things the lady on the advertising posters was. She had refused to shower that evening in fear of washing it away. Two months later, on her eighteenth birthday, it was finally hers.

She had placed it on her bathroom shelf so that she could admire it every single day. Every morning she saw it as she went to brush her teeth, every evening she saw it before she went to bed. It was magnificent − something she would never dare to buy herself, she would never be so self indulgent, never reward herself with such opulence. She would make do with the cut price fragrances in the supermarket or the body sprays that cost next to nothing but made her feel glamorous, if only for an hour or so. She would wear it one day though, for a special occasion, someday soon – that's what she was waiting for, so that she could wear it and feel special and beautiful. One day.

So there it sat, on the shelf, looking perfect. It sat there for years, until the vibrant colours of the box were dulled by the sunlight and the contents had almost given up hope of being released.

Eventually, she decided it might be time. She stepped out of the shower, shoulders glistening with beads of water dripping from her hair. There was no occasion, but the box had been there so long that it was starting to look neglected and she needed reminding of the promise it held inside. She pulled down the box from the shelf and blew the layer of dust that had made its home on the lid. She squinted her eyes as she tried to make out the faded pattern. The bottle slid out into her hand, she didn't ever remember it being so dark in colour. But it *had* been a few years since she had taken the bottle out, and memories, like dreams, do tend to fade over time. She lifted her chin to spray and caught a glimpse of someone staring back at her. The reflection made her stop for a moment. She recognised the face. A few years ago this face would have been so excited to do what she was about to do. But the reflection was no longer a fresh faced 18 year old with all the excitement of life ahead of her.

She let her finger press down - she wasn't entirely sure if the scent would appeal to her now she was older, so she sprayed it, carefully, gently, being careful not to waste it. But it wasn't the same, she didn't get that same sense of excitement and glamour. She just smelt a rather old, musty idea of special.

The special occasions didn't arrive and the perfume sat unused. She never did get to indulge herself. She never did replace the perfume. And now when she saw the bottle on the shelf it made her feel sad, sad for the loss of a dream, sad for the lack of opportunity to wear it. Sad.

12

Again

She curled up in a ball, covering her face with an old t-shirt in an attempt to block out the smell that infused her sheets. This was supposed to be her safe place, her place of comfort, a place of warmth. She thought she would feel safe there, secure, wanted. He'd spent a while tempting her, giving her an idea of what it would be like, promising her the earth. She had listened, taking it all in, slowly believing it all. She was an intelligent girl, she's heard the boys try to talk their way through her defences before. But he was different. He had listened to her, not talked at her, and he made her feel wanted and appreciated. He was different. She had decided to share her safe space with him. But she had invited him in and now she felt broken.

She turned over away from the light escaping through the slight gap between the curtains. She wanted to hide herself, repulsed by the flashbacks she had in her head. At this moment in time, she hated herself, she hated how he had made her feel. Her excitement and anticipation was short lived and she soon realised that she was just a prop, a prop to make him feel better.

As quickly as he had come to her, his attentiveness had vanished. His softly spoken compliments were replaced with short, sharp responses and, once he had removed himself from her, the compliments quickly disappeared. Wasn't this what she wanted? It wasn't supposed to be like this. Not in her head. No, she knew this wasn't what she wanted, she wanted, no, she deserved more.

He had left soon after, leaving her with a promise of a text and a sense of self-loathing that made her physically sick. She sat up and covered her face with her hands. She didn't want to see herself in the mirror; she didn't want to see herself at all. She showered with her eyes closed, letting the water wash over her, knowing that it would take much more than water to wash away how she felt.

She didn't get a text. She didn't even check her phone. She wasn't sure she would respond to him even if he did try to contact her. She tidied her hair, put on her lip gloss and took a deep breath. 'Next time' she thought, 'next time will be different'. Her flicker of optimism pulled her briefly out from the depths of self loathing. In spite of herself, she lived in hope that she would find a man whose sole intent was not to invade her safe space. She changed the sheets, opened the window and took a deep breath.

Time to face the world again she told herself.

13

Chip Shop Friendship

I'm not sure when I decided I didn't like her. I think it may have been when she farted in the chip shop and blamed me. She was always doing things like that. I told her that she would never find a boyfriend if she kept behaving like that but she just shrugged her shoulders and flicked her hair. She didn't care, unlike me, I cared about everything. I wouldn't leave the house if my hair didn't fall in the right way, if I had a spot I would go into hiding until it became less conspicuous. She wouldn't care about things like that, she floated through life like the wind, like one great big fart, making people laugh and disgusting them in equal measures.

She flitted past mirrors without so much as a second glance and quite often grabbed her hair and threw it into a ponytail without checking if it looked OK afterwards. Her cheeks were always that perfect shade pink with life, and her eyes had a natural spark that made them look like they might ignite. She didn't obsess about make-up or fake tan. She was alive. She breathed excitement. I felt like a doll when I was with her, fake, plastic, rigid. She danced like the sun on the ocean whereas I felt like slimy weeds on the shore, redundant and gross.

She was the one who always knew what to say just at the exact right time. She didn't need any help in fitting in with a crown or looking effortlessly beautiful. She had the face of an angel, and then now and again, she'd swear. Not a little swear, but a big fat disgusting one. And she would laugh, wickedly, as if she knew how shocking she had been. And then she danced away. Skipping. Laughing. And I would be left behind, red faced and awkward. I hated it when she did that.

If I am honest, I'm not sure if I didn't like her, or if I didn't like how I could never be like her. She was free. Unique. She stood out in a crowd where I blended in, the wallpaper friend, the one who was there to make up the numbers. But I didn't disgust anyone, not with my actions anyway, and I'm going to cling on to that. And boys don't like disgusting girls do they? They like girls who blush, and don't fart. Yes, I'll stay away from her, from her flowing hair and her sparking eyes. And her farts.

14

Small Talk

'I absolutely 100% do not find Tom Jones attractive' exclaimed Samantha as she poured the last of the wine bottle into her glass. '100%. Absolutely not.'

Max turned his head to look at her, eyebrow raised. He stared at her for a minute and then turned away. He had no idea why she thought he would suspect her of such a crush.

'Are you listening Max? Did you hear me? Did you hear what I said? Because I don't. I absolutely do not fancy him. I know I had that dream about him, remember that dream? Well it was just a dream. It doesn't mean that I actually fancy him does it? I mean, I dream about lots of people. Doesn't mean I want to run off with them does it?' She took another sip of the supermarket brand wine.

Max didn't respond. He let his eyes close slowly, blocking out Samantha's constant jabbering. She often did this after a bottle of wine. Last week it was Simon Cowell and a bottle of Pinot

Grigio. It had become a ritual on a Friday night, work clothes off, night clothes on, mobile off, TV on, Facebook closed, wine bottle opened. Max had already been sitting for a couple of hours listening to her.

'And I tell you something else Max, I bloody love you I do'.

And she meant it. She adored Max. Ever since she invited him into her home she never had any regrets, not one. She loved the way he would be there to greet her after a day at work, how he'd playfully wake her in the morning for some attention. She loved the fact that there was another heartbeat in the house.

Max got up. He'd had enough. He couldn't listen to this any longer. He got up and made his way to the back door. It was Friday night, he was too young to be stuck in all night, he couldn't cope with another night listening to her – another hour and she'd start crying, telling him that he was all she had, making him promise not to leave her all alone. She needed to get a grip of herself, find herself some friends, get herself out there. He waited for a minute by the door. Samantha had followed him into the kitchen and was in the fridge searching for more wine, muttering to herself.

'Go on then, go out, I don't care. I suppose you'll be out all night, don't worry about me, I'll be OK here, all on my own, again.'

Max stared at her as she held her hand to her forehead dramatically. She caught his eye and her face softened slightly. She moved over towards him, and placed her hand on his face and kissed him. She opened the door,

'go on then, off you go.'

Max left the house and didn't even look back. Samantha closed

the door and smiled to herself,
   'I still love you, you daft cat'.

15

Make Up

She'd always come across as being a bit moody, that girl on the bus. I'd watch her every morning, layering on makeup to her already perfect face. I don't know why girls feel the need to do that. She looks perfectly fine without it to me. More than fine in fact. Her mirror wasn't quite big enough to fit her whole face in so she would move it around, checking each part in turn, her eyes, her nose, her cheeks. It was a fascinating process. She caught me watching her one morning and snapped her mirror shut with such venom that I was sure she had just bought herself seven years of bad luck. She had asked me what I was staring at, but I didn't answer her. It wasn't really a question that required a response.

She was one of the popular girls at school, she hung around with the girls who had time to do their hair and makeup in the morning, the girls who spent their weekends hanging around the park waiting for the boys with cars. I didn't have a car. I had a bike. Girls like that didn't look at boys like me.

When she got off the bus at the end of the day, she always waited until it had pulled away and then got out a packet of wipes from her bag. Her little mirror came back out and she wiped that girl away. Just like that, in seconds. And then she was that little girl that I remember from primary school, the one who used to beg me to give her a ride on my bike, the one who used to share her sweets with me. The pretty girl with the electric blue eyes and rose tinted lips, the days before she started high school, before she felt the need to paint her face on in the mornings. I liked her, she was nice.

We don't really talk much any more. It's a shame because there is so much that I would like to say to her. She wouldn't want to hear it, she had no interest in me. She wouldn't want to hear me tell her that I think she looked much better without her mask, that I found her eyes enchanting, that her lips were the nicest shade of pink that I had ever seen. I wanted to hear her story, I wanted to know why she painted her face every morning. I wanted to know, even more, why she had to take it off every night. Maybe her dad didn't like it. Dads are protective over their little girls aren't they? Maybe that was it. She didn't seem so little with that mask on. But I could see it. I could see that little girl still trapped behind that made up face, and I wanted to know her. I wish she would let me see her.

* * *

She scooped up her hair into a ponytail being careful to pull out a few strands at the sides. She liked a bit of camouflage. Those little strands of hair stopped the world from seeing her naked face. Well, as naked as it can be with a layer of No7 Golden Beige and a few coats of Extra Black Volumising mascara - her mask to face the world. She often looked at women who wore no makeup with envy. She wished she was confident enough to face the world without any war paint. She wished she didn't care what people thought about her. She would often look at herself in the mirror, tracing the outline with her finger, admiring the crystal blue of her eyes and her English rose complexion. She was a pretty girl, her small features gave her a doll-like quality and her lips were a shade of pink that no cosmetic company had ever managed to capture. She was classically pretty. And every morning she covered up her face with a chemical based one; her natural beauty suffocating below a mask of no-crease, no slide, no fade makeup.

She was 14 when she started to cover her face. She did it at first because everyone else was doing it, she didn't want to stand out, she didn't want to be different, so every morning, at the bus stop, she stood with a small compact mirror and created her new face. And every evening, when she got off the bus, she stood again, with her compact mirror and a pack of makeup remover wipes. Her mother would never let her leave the house wearing make-up. She said it would make her attract the wrong sort of attention, that she would look cheap. Secretly she wished she would get some attention, other than the constant nagging and the comments about how she'd never be good enough. And she really did want the boys to notice her, because at least then she would feel special.

She was a popular girl, whilst she wore her mask. She was confident, fiery, and intriguing. She got so used to being that girl that she forgot what the girl underneath was looking for. And before she knew it, it was too late. She was alone. She started to resent the girl who lay beneath the surface, the pretty girl, the girl with a voice and ideas and a heart. She didn't have the confidence to let her out any more. No-one she knew would probably even remember her true face. So she only appeared at night, in the mirror, staring at herself, wishing she could be seen, wishing someone would see her.

16

Unopened

On the morning of Wednesday 10th September 2014, at precisely 6.24am, Anna Lewis, being of sound body and mind, sat on an ornate iron patio chair in her south facing garden wearing nothing but her blue cotton striped pyjamas, holding in her hand an unopened letter.

It had been an unusually warm summer. The grass was scorched in places, the cracked earth under the weave of yellow tinged grass groaned for rain. The garden wall radiated heat even in the early hours and the morning air breathed a cool sigh before the sun pierced through and overpowered it. The morning birds had greeted the dawn with a riotous chorus and they now let the humming bees and lawnmowers take their part in the symphony.

It wasn't unusual for Anna to be in the garden, she had spent most of the summer there, the perk of being a teacher. She wasn't a particularly keen gardener but she knew how to edge a lawn and prune a clematis. But today was different. Today she didn't see the dancing bees on the honeysuckle that grew along her wall, today she didn't feel the dew on her bare feet. Today, just for this moment, she let the world carry on around her.

Anna hadn't been shocked when she heard the rattle of the letterbox at 6 that morning. The post had been delivered earlier than usual over the past few weeks, Anna guessed the postman would want to get it done before the heat got too much. As she came down the stairs, she saw the envelope on the mat. The sun was throwing prisms of light around the oak flooring as it shone through the bevelled glass in the front door. Anna loved her front door. Not because it was particularly expensive, or even fancy, but because it kept the world out. It was the door to her safe place, her haven. Every night after work it was there when she pulled on her drive, opening only to her. Every morning as she closed it behind her she took comfort in the knowledge she would be opening it again soon. It was a black door, composite with the highest level locking mechanism. It had a British standard kite mark. She had checked. She had made sure it was the most secure door you could buy without going to an industrial supplier. When she closed and locked that door, nothing would get through it, nothing except for her – and her post.

Anna had picked up the envelope amongst the charity clothing bag and the free weekly newspaper as she walked through into her gleaming white kitchen. She flicked through the pile slowly, raising her eyebrows with interest as she came across the handwritten envelope. She filled the kettle and switched it on robotically and set herself down at the oak kitchen table as she waited for it to boil. She turned the envelope over in her hand slowly admiring the idea that someone had taken the time to sit down and write to her. She used to get handwritten appointment letters from her dentist. Beryl, the receptionist, had worked there all her life and handwritten appointment letters were how she had always done it, absolutely no point in changing things around now, absolutely no point whatsoever. Over her dead body apparently. Ironic really as she died a couple of weeks after she retired and they had moved over to a computerised system the very next week.

No, she knew it wasn't from the dentist, and her birthday had been months before so not a belated card of apology either. She poured the freshly boiled water into one of her 'world's best teacher' mugs, still holding the letter in her other hand. The whole idea of a handwritten letter appealed to Anna's romantic side. Someone somewhere in the world has thought about me, has sat down with a pen and written a letter, thinking carefully about each word that spills out from the pen. She looked out of the window wistfully, the sun lighting up half of her face and filling her with warmth. She sighed, picked up her coffee and sat at the table.

In another life she would have panicked about receiving a letter like this in case it was bad news. Perhaps news of a death in the family or close friend. But as the years went by, the family circle diminished until there was no one of any significance left. Her close friends were no longer close, physically or emotionally, but then life was busy and she was busy and everything was busy. Old friends stopped contacting her a long time ago. Maybe she wouldn't open it. Maybe she would shred it along with the

65

old bank statements. Did she need to know what was inside it? Could she bear to destroy it before she read its contents?

And so she went out to the garden, in her pyjamas with the unopened letter in her hand.

The truth was, deep down, she knew what was in the letter. She knew that this was a letter from someone who she had known about for many years, many many years, long before her husband, Allan had died. As she stared at the cursive writing she knew she recognised it from gift tags and cards that had been stashed under the mattress – items from another life that she wasn't supposed to be part of. She was never going to open the letter because she didn't need to know what was in it, too much time had passed and she had made peace with how her life had panned out. There was nothing in that letter that would change that, she wouldn't let it. There was no point bringing it all back up again, not now, not now he was gone.

It was time she acted though, it was time she finally put this to bed. She being of sound mind, in fact, being of sounder mind than she had ever been in her life, Anna walked back into the house, picked up the urn from the mantelpiece, carried it out to the garden and emptied the lot in the compost bin. She then threw the letter in on top. There you go, now you can both rot in hell.

17

Blue Flowers

He watched her as she walked down the street. He often saw her at this time, he assumed she was on a break from work. She would walk down one side of the street to the old post office before she crossed over and then would walk back up the other side. Just after the betting shop she would cross back over the road and go back into the office building. It took her 11 minutes, sometimes 12 depending on where she crossed over and what the traffic was doing.

Today she was wearing a black coat, the first time for a coat this year, it looked nice. She looked nice in black. Through the summer she would wear all colours, he liked blue the best. The blue top with the little flowers on. The kind of blue he imagined her eyes were, not that he had ever seen her eyes; he'd never been that close to her. But he imagined they were the blue of the sea on a summer's day when the sky reflected off the water or a field of cornflowers alive with the breath of the breeze. She never had a bag with her; she didn't want to buy anything, nor did she need her makeup. He liked that, she was a free spirit, just walking, minding her own business not needing anything or anyone.

She had already gone down the sunnier side of the street. The sunlight reflected off her hair the same way that it bounced off the bonnet of a car. Her hair was almost too shiny, if that were possible. She had crossed over outside the old post office, avoiding the uneven pavement where the postbox once stood, and was making her way back up toward him. This was his favourite bit. He could see her head on, and he often imagined she was coming to meet him, coming to tell him she loved him, or just coming to say 'hi'. She never did though. She never even saw him. This side of the street was dull, unappealing, boarded up shops and litter strewn pavements. She was like an angel, albeit an angel in a black coat, sashaying along without a care in the world, bringing light to an otherwise dark day.

She stopped way before the betting shop today. She didn't normally stop there. She normally crossed after the betting shop. I don't know why she crossed there today. That was her mistake. That was where she went wrong. She just misjudged it. There was something blocking her. By the time she stepped out it was over, nothing could be done. For a moment there was complete silence, like the world stopped briefly to acknowledge her soul before the wild noise of trauma began.

He never saw her again, but he laid some flowers there whenever he could. Blue ones.

18

Sausage Fingers

They both sat there, in silence. She could see him stabbing at the screen of his mobile phone. She watched him, his finger swiping across the screen like a fat sausage, a fat pork sausage oozing with fat and grease. She turned away in disgust. She hated that he had put on so much weight. She hated the fact that he didn't care, even more. Just another thing that added to her ever increasing list of things she despised about him lately.

At least she made an effort; at least she actually cared about what she looked like, or at least tried. She would purposely choose something healthy off the menu when they ate out, as if to shame him into substituting his chips for a salad or to skip dessert. It only seemed to make him worse. Then she would be starving when they got in and she would sneak into the kitchen and grab a handful of biscuits or a packet of crisps and then lock herself in the bathroom to eat them.

She hated her body almost as much as she hated his. She hated how he never noticed when she lost a pound or squeezed into her size 10 jeans. He didn't see it. He didn't see her any more, he just saw the woman he lived with, not the woman he fell in love with. She often wondered if he still loved her, she often wondered if she ever loved him.

It was all so easy when they first met. Their mutual friends had thrown them together and it just seemed the convenient thing to do. It made the dinner party table plans easier, wedding seating plans more convenient and the couples weekends away cheaper. Convenience, that's all, and she wondered if love had ever entered the equation. She couldn't even remember the last time he told her that he loved her. There was an occasional ruffling of the hair and a 'you're a good 'un' but not a 'I love you', not a 'you mean the world to me', just a smack on the arse and a 'fancy a quickie'. No. She didn't fancy a quickie. Not at all. She turned away to stare at the TV screen.

She wondered what other couples did in the evenings, normal couples, couples that loved each other. She wondered if they were like those adverts for sofas where the wife sat in her nice clothes watching the baby play on the clean carpet and the husband suddenly appears and puts his hand on her shoulder and they share a look that says 'look at our perfect life. No doubt he then takes her to bed and makes love to her all night (after making sure the baby was fed and washed and fast asleep). And then gets up and makes her a cup of tea. And wipes up after him. And puts the milk back in the fridge. Or even goes to the garage to make sure there is enough milk for the morning. A whole world away from what was happening right now. Sausage fingers engrossed in the rugby results on his phone and her clinging on to fake lives on sofa adverts.

She got up and walked to the kitchen, not entirely sure what for but anything to move the air around the room. She flicked on the kitchen light and automatically switched the kettle on to boil. She went through the routine: two mugs from the draining board, the one with purple owls for her, which read 'tea time twit twoo' and the green one with the rather handsome cartoon rugby player that said 'nice try'. It wouldn't even be so bad if he played rugby, but he just watched it, whilst stuffing pies down his neck and washing them down with beer from plastic cups. She swilled the mugs out under the tap and placed them next to the kettle. Maybe she was to blame. Maybe she should make more of an effort – What was stopping her from going on there right now and suggesting they go to the pub, for out for tea, or the cinema – something, anything rather than sit, stagnant, counting down the minutes until the house was silent again due to sleep and not to either of them not speaking. Maybe that's what she would do right now.

The kettle came to the boil and the switch popped out. No, she would just take him some tea and go up and have a bath. The pub would mean he would get drunk, and god forbid he might try for some sexy time when they got back. Yuk. No thanks. A meal would mean that she would have to sit by him and listen to him eating. She considered the cinema, but then couldn't justify spending money to sit in silence when they did a perfectly good job of doing that at home every night. – for free. Or maybe she would just open a bottle of wine instead of making tea. They could both have a drink, maybe she would feel like being a little bit more intimate with him if she'd had a drink, and he wouldn't get too drunk as there was only one bottle in the house. She checked the fridge. No, the wine bottle was gone. Again. She reached for the milk, reverting back to robotic mode, annoyed with herself for even thinking of changing the routine.

She slid the coaster along the table and set the mug of tea next to him. His sausage finger paused for a second, and then continued swiping. 'You're welcome' she muttered to herself as she shook her head slowly. He looked up at her. 'Ta' he replied. Not even a 'ta love'. She took her drink upstairs, slamming the bathroom door behind her.

* * *

He hated it when she did that – why not just tell him what was up with her? Why slam the door? She was so moody lately, she hardly ever struck up conversation, or smiled, or anything. Lying next to her in bed was as comforting as a paper cut in a vinegar factory. She was so distant, so cold. He had often wondered if she was having an affair, but the fact that she spent most of her time on the sofa watching TV told him otherwise. If she wanted a new sofa all she had to do was ask, she didn't have to keep putting on those adverts every ten minutes. I can get the hint. She spends so long sitting on it that it's no wonder she's considering a new one. She never used to be so lazy. We used to do stuff together all the time, but she hates rugby and all of our friends are having children. I'd take her out for a meal now and again but all she does is tut at me and tell me I'm making too much noise when I eat. Or breathe. I swear my breathing repulses her. I'd stop if I could – she'd like that.

I'm sure she hates the way that I look too, she's always making comments like 'are you eating - AGAIN?' I'm not sure why it bothers her so much. Graham, my brother has put on lots of weight over the years and his wife, Mandy still thinks he's fit, she tells us the time, especially after a glass of wine. They still laugh together. Maybe she's just worried about my health, of course. But there's no need for her to be so cruel. She could just leave me. I'd be sad, of course I would, but if I am making her that miserable then just go and be happy somewhere else. But then again, that would mean she'd have to get off the sofa. She's in the bath now, and then she'll get straight into bed. She'll pretend to be asleep when I get in, or she'll roll over so she doesn't have to look at me. She's not so perfect herself. She's put quite a bit of weight on over the past few years, but she still looks great - she is great. But she's just so bloody miserable.

I've been looking for holidays on my phone tonight, it's our anniversary soon, I have a feeling it's make or break so I want to take her somewhere special, somewhere away from the rugby and the sofa – I'd never keep anything from her, if she asked me what she was doing then I would tell her, but she was annoyed about making me a cup of tea, a cup of tea that I never asked her to make. Ah that could be it actually, I didn't say thank you, but I was scared she was going to see what was on my phone. I'd better apologise to her. I'll go up in a minute – maybe take her a glass of wine. There's a bottle in the boot of the car I bought on the way home from work to replace the one she drank the other week. She does that a lot, drinks the wine then has a strop that it isn't in the fridge.

He got up and unlocked the front door to go out to the car. It had been raining so he ran across the pavement as if it was on fire so as not to get his socks wet. They lived on a busy street – she had insisted they be close to town so they could walk to the coffee shops, like proper grown up couples. But the coffee shop had closed down and now the road was used as a rat run to get to the motorway. Cars zoomed alone there like greyhounds after the rabbit. He'd parked across the other side of the read this evening as Julie at number 28 had her evening caller around. He stabbed at the car with his remote and it winked to life. He opened the boot and took out the carrier bag containing the wine bottle. Red, her favourite. He'd splashed out on the good stuff this evening, a Nero D'Avola. He briefly recalled the Sicilian vineyard they had visited on their honeymoon. It felt like another lifetime. How far apart they had become since they first cemented their love with a ring. He shut the boot and gave it an extra try to make sure it was closed properly; he was careful like that. Thorough. She'd say he was over the top. Too cautious. Boring.

He had looked back at the house after he closed the car boot. It looked so cosy from the outside. The windows threw out a golden honey glow and the front door, all red and shiny, looked inviting. How ironic, he thought to himself. The house inside could have been made out of steel for how warm and comforting it felt to him. He lifted his face to the rain and felt the raindrops fall onto his skin and breathed in deeply. He suddenly felt alive and free, each raindrop injecting a bit of hope into him. The air was cold and fresh and he could feel his whole body relax. He wasn't going to give up on her just yet, their story wasn't finished quite yet. Yes, he'd march with purpose back into that house and get their relationship back on track, right across the road, right across that very very busy road, in the rain, in the dark.

* * *

She lay in the bath, in two minds whether to get out and take a look at what was going on outside the window. There was always some commotion going on in that street. The cars drove too fast, people double parked, it was a nightmare. She had such high hopes for it when they moved in, the estate agent talked about regeneration and café culture. It hadn't materialised and they were stuck in commuter hell. She lay back in the water, he'd come stomping up the stairs in a minute to tell her the news. She sighed at the thought of having to feign interest, of having to talk to him. He was so dull. So so dull. She swirled the water around in the bath and closed her eyes.

But he didn't come. She let the warm water and the bubbles surround her and she lay there, thankful.

* * *

Julie, at number 28, rushed out of her front door closely followed by her gentleman friend. They had heard the sickening bang and the ferocious screeching of tyres over the quiet hum of the TV. Outside the rain fell heavily and the air was thick with the smell of rubber and oil and fear. He should have really been more careful crossing back over the road.

19

Time Out

There is a feeling that comes with silence, a sort of nervous anxiousness that surrounds us like an early morning mist, and we never quite know what the day ahead will bring. The absence of sound signals to the brain that now is the time to start doing that thing that brains do when there is silence; the thinking that occurs when there's nothing to think about, the thoughts that appear when we have nothing else to distract them with. These are the times that I cannot fear but cannot enjoy. These are the times that I have to give in to myself.

As I sit here, in silence, I can hear my breath, carrying life enabling oxygen around my body, keeping me alive. Maybe now would be a good time to try a deep breathing exercise. In for 5, out for 5. Immediately, I feel my heart leap into action and my breathing becomes quicker. Oh God here we go, I think I'm panicking again. How am I the only person in the world who hears 'breathing exercise' and suddenly loses the ability to breathe normally. Maybe that's the point, maybe the point is that I am not normal. Am I normal? Am I having the same thoughts as everyone else but am unaware as you can't see other people's thoughts? I'm thinking about the lady who works on reception in the local library. She said something the other week that made me wonder if she was normal. Can't actually recall what it was, maybe something to do with enjoying crime novels a little too much. I reckon she has the potential to be a secret criminal. I wonder what criminals think of when it's silent – I wonder if it ever gets silent in prison? I imagine there's always something going on. I watched a documentary once about spending 24 hours in prison. It seemed quite chaotic to me.

That reminds me, I need to do a food shop. I wonder if my food shop is similar to everyone else's. Do people buy the same things each week or is every week a lucky dip – 'ooh I'll pick up one of these this week', or 'we've not had that before, let's give it a whirl'. I tend to be more of a 'we need this, this and this'. Seems quite boring in comparison. Perhaps I'll mix it up this week and buy something new. Irish sausages instead of pork maybe. I've never been to Ireland. I wonder if in Ireland, Irish sausages are just called sausages? I like sausages, especially between 2 pieces of bread. Would I say they are my favourite food? I'm not sure I would. What is my favourite food? I'm not sure I have one. If someone asked me what my favourite food was, what would I say? Shit, I need an answer in case someone asks me. Cheesecake? I like cheesecake, but not all cheesecakes, only certain sorts. No bake cheesecakes perhaps. Does that make me sound fussy? I'm not fussy, am I? I should stick to something less fussy really. Bread? No, that makes me sound boring. Maybe just cake. Cake can cover a range of things can't it? Not a huge fan of chocolate cake though, which is strange really as I like chocolate.

Can't remember the last time I ate any chocolate to be honest. I think it was a bounty that I picked up from the garage last week when I forgot to press the 'pay at pump' option. I didn't really want to go inside as my old next-door neighbour worked there and I never really liked her. I wonder if she liked me or said to her colleague 'urgh, you serve this next one, I used to live next door to her and she's a cow'. Anyway, it was irrelevant because she wasn't there and I felt compelled to pick up a Bounty from the display at the till. Hate having to go inside. Remember when there was no such thing as pay at pump and drive throughs? I sound like my mum 'when I was younger...'. How young is 'younger'? Am I classed as old now? 46? Is that middle aged – what are the thresholds in this situation? I guess I'm more middle-aged than old aged aren't I? No, I am definitely not old. But my God how did that happen? Seems like yesterday that I left school.

Should have concentrated more at school really, could have made something more with my life. You can do anything if you put your mind to it, they say. They - whoever 'they' are. I put my mind to passing all of my GCSEs but it turned out that my mind wasn't quite up to speed with that notion so I'm not sure how true that statement is. Won't be the first person to fail them, won't be the last either I imagine. Imagine being the first person to fail an exam, what a responsibility – paving the way for those who fail. Sounds like the title I'd be in with a shot of claiming. I'd be hailed by all those with academically challenged brains and scorned by those who are in the 'you can achieve anything' camp. I've not done too bad though I reckon; I've got a job that pays the bills. Speaking of which, what's the time, I should really get back to it. Yes, this half hour or relaxing and switching off has really helped. I must do it again sometime.

20

The Wait

Emma sat at her kitchen table. The harsh fluorescent lighting bounded off the gleaming white surfaces, throwing an unhealthy pale glow on her cheeks. She had spent all morning cleaning that kitchen. All morning scrubbing at the floor and wiping down the windows – and now it shone. Now it was almost too clean. Now it made her feel uneasy sitting in such a clinical, sterile room. Now her nostrils were stinging with the smell of bleach and her hands were almost raw from the boiling water. Her body now sat rigid at the table, stiff, only her rising and falling chest signalling that she was still alive. She let a solitary tear roll down her cheek but did not dare wipe it away for fear of moving the air.

It took all her energy to breath; with each rise of her chest she could taste the chemicals and with each exhalation she feared she had let too much of herself back in the room. She could leave. She could get up and go right now. Just into the next room, anywhere. But her body was frozen to the seat. Her body refused to move and her mind didn't have the energy to force it. She wondered how long she could sit there before someone would notice she wasn't around. She wondered how long a clean kitchen would stay clean if no one ever used it again.

The previous evening, Emma had stood in front of the full length bedroom mirror and admired herself. Despite missing her last two appointments, her dark brown hair shone and bounced around her shoulders, her natural curl emitting an air of effortless perfection. She had applied her make up carefully, trying very hard to make herself look more sexy than she felt. Her lipstick was new, a shade brighter than she would normally dare to wear, and she had used a scented moisturiser as well as perfume. She hadn't felt like she had made this much effort since her 16th birthday party. She hadn't needed to. She hadn't ever considered that someone may find her attractive, either with or without makeup, and so she hadn't bothered. And if she was honest, she didn't really feel that she knew what to do with a skin highlighter or a contour kit. But tonight she wanted to feel like she was in control, that she knew how to be a woman. She wanted him to see that she could play a sexy woman about town as easily as the girl next door. She just wanted to feel something.

She turned sideways to make sure she still looked good from another angle. She did. The black dress was not her usual style and the lace scratched her arms. Her small frame made her feel like a child, but her underwear had helped her look like a woman in all of the right places. She had brought high heeled shoes to make her look taller. She was happy with what she saw.

She sat down on the edge of the bed, being careful not to disturb the pristinely ironed bed covers, and got her thoughts together.

Her mouth was dry and her heart was pounding. She checked the time on her phone. He would be there to collect her in 25 minutes. She scanned around her bedroom. She had hidden her teddy bears and the photo of her at Disneyland. She had cleared away her spot control cream and her Mickey Mouse pyjamas and had stashed her medication away. It looked like a grown-up's bedroom and she looked like a woman.

She took a deep breath. She put herself under so much pressure all of the time. This man was never going to see the inside of her bedroom so she really had no need to stage it so precisely. But she felt that it added to the whole façade. She may look like a woman, but inside she felt like a girl on Christmas Eve. Tonight she was going on a date, with a man, a man who openly admitted that he thought she was attractive and alluring. She had sent him photos and he had been impressed. He was a teacher. He was respectable. She trusted him.

She hadn't told her friends or the clinic she was meeting him this evening. She wasn't sure how they would react and she didn't want anyone to tell her that she wasn't strong enough. She wasn't even sure it would sound the same if she said the words out loud. In her head it all made sense. OK, so they hadn't actually met in real life, but he had told her things, personal things, intimate things. He wouldn't do that if he didn't think there was a future between them. He had asked her questions, had listened to her answers; he was genuinely interested in her. When he asked if she wanted to meet up he hadn't put any pressure on her – 'in your own time,' he had said. ' No rush'. The last time he had asked her she had declined, through nerves, but then he had disappeared for a few days and she feared he'd had second thoughts. She had felt a bit lost when he wasn't responding to her messages and she didn't want him to lose interest, so she had told him she would meet him. He had offered to pick her up and she debated about telling him where she lived, but he told her that it would be easier than walking into a bar or restaurant on her own. He didn't want her to feel uncomfortable and he said he wanted to walk in with her on his arm, to show her off to everyone. Emma thought that was very thoughtful and romantic. And he was a teacher after all - he had a respectable job, and teachers have all sorts of checks nowadays so it was perfectly safe.

She made her way down the stairs very carefully, negotiating her new heels on each step and breathed a sigh of relief when she got to the bottom. She could see the front door at the end of the hallway and her stomach lurched. She would be answering that door soon, and he would be there. She made her way into the kitchen. It was clean and tidy and the kettle was full of water, just in case he wanted a drink before they went. She had even bought new mugs; she lined them up with all the handles pointing in the same direction. She popped her head around the living room door just to check it was respectable. She hadn't been in there since getting in from work as she had gone straight upstairs to get ready. She hadn't planned on him going in there either – they could sit at the kitchen table if he wanted a coffee. That was respectable. That's what grown-ups do after a first date.

She closed the blinds in the kitchen window so that she wasn't in full view from the street. She didn't want him to think she was waiting there for him. She would answer the door as if she had just thrown on her outfit – she wanted him to think that this look wasn't too hard to achieve.

Five minutes later there was a knock on the door. It startled Emma. She had been expecting to see headlights shine through the blinds first – that was to have been her warning that he was here. But she hadn't seen any headlights. Maybe it wasn't him? She debated peeping through the blinds to check, but decided it would make her look nervous and unsure, so she took a deep breath and walked, as confidently as she could in heels, to answer the door.

He hadn't driven to her house that evening, he had arrived in a taxi and he stood at her front door with flowers and a bottle of wine. She wasn't sure what to do in this situation, it felt wrong to take the bottle and not offer him a glass. So she invited him in and before he had a chance to even have the opportunity to say no, she had poured them both a glass. A glass of wine would settle her nerves, she thought. She'd drink it slowly, she didn't want to appear giggly too soon and she was never quite sure how her medication would react with it. In any case, more than two glasses of wine usually made her sick, and she couldn't let that happen. She was also disappointed that they wouldn't have that journey in the car to break the ice, to get the nerves out of the way. But it was too late now; he was there, in front of her. He was dressed smartly but he wasn't clean shaven. Emma had expected him to be clean shaven. Why hadn't he had a shave? She told herself not to be so fussy. Real women aren't fussy. Stop it Emma.

She was suddenly wrenched from her thoughts by the sound of a phone ringing. The vibrations of the device made it edge away from the safety of the shelf and it fell to the floor. As it landed on the tiled floor, the cover came away and the battery flew out, plummeting the room back into silence. The gleaming tiles were now infected with shards of plastic. Emma watched it all happen. She didn't move. She didn't want to know who had phoned her, she didn't want to speak to anyone. It wasn't like she needed help – she was fine, she was alive.

He should have driven, he should have picked her up and taken her straight out. He shouldn't have brought wine. She shouldn't have poured such large glasses. There were lots of things that shouldn't have happened that evening. She shouldn't have made out she was as confident as she was. She should have been honest about herself on her profile. They shouldn't have stayed in the kitchen. There are dangerous things in the kitchen. She shouldn't have pulled him into her when she really wanted to push him away. She shouldn't have told him she wanted him when she didn't. She shouldn't have panicked when he tried to kiss her. She shouldn't have panicked. She should have said no. She could have said stop. He would have done it. He would have listened. He would have stopped. If she had only said no...

He had left that evening with more than a wounded heart. It did, however, look more dramatic than it was. It had all happened so quickly. It had all been going so well. She had changed, in the space of five seconds, her eyes had gone from alluring to scared. He had tried to pull away but she had pulled him into her. He hadn't seen her hand reaching behind her. He hadn't seen her grab the nearest thing. How different it would have been if she had grabbed a spatula. He smiled and winced at the same time. A flesh wound maybe, but it didn't make it any less painful. He sat in the waiting room with his head in his hands, not sure if he felt sick due to the shock, the pain or the smell of disinfectant and stale vomit. He had a million thoughts bounding around, like five year olds on a sugar high, all screaming and jumping and refusing to stand still. He couldn't make sense of it all despite replaying the evening again and again in his head. Had she told him no? Had he not heard her? Yes, he had had a drink but he wasn't drunk. He knew exactly what was going on – and she hadn't drunk that much. He wouldn't have let it get too far if she had - he had a sister for god's sake, he would never put someone in that position. She had told him that she wanted him. She had said that it was OK, she trusted him. He put his head in his hands and waited for his name to be called.

He had managed to convince them that it was just a silly accident, the sort you have when you've drunk too much wine. He didn't want her to get into trouble for this. He wanted the situation to disappear. The nurse had laughed at him when he said he felt faint. She had teased him for being a wuss. Twenty-four hours earlier he would have considered that young nurse was flirting with him. Now he wasn't taking any chances and he lowered his gaze to the floor. She stitched him up.

Emma waited for someone to knock at the door. She was waiting for someone to come and take her away. She wanted the kitchen to be clean when they got there. She wanted the mess cleaned up. She couldn't leave it like that. But no one knocked at the door. No one came.

After realising that no one was coming for her, Emma let her legs carry her weight and she got up from the table. She moved the knife block back into its proper place. She took the fourth glass from the right out of the cabinet and filled it with water three times before finally taking a sip and swallowing her four tablets. All in the correct order. She washed and dried the glass and put it straight back where it belonged before making her way back to the safety of her bedroom. She closed the door behind her, her nose relieved to breathe in air that wasn't polluted with chemicals and fear. She opened her bedside drawer and took out the picture of herself at Disneyland and put it back in its place on her dressing table. She was wearing a pair of Mickey Mouse ears, dressing up to make herself feel like someone else. Just like on her sixteenth birthday. Just like that night in the kitchen. She climbed into her bed, pulling the covers tight around her, cocooning herself in warmth and safety.

She was woken up by the vibrating of her phone. She lay on her back, looking at the ceiling and let it divert to voicemail. She wasn't going to answer it, she didn't want to talk to anyone. A rush of panic prickled over her skin, *what if it was them? What if they were coming to take me away?* She deserved to be punished for what she did. She lay, motionless, her thoughts invading her head. 'What have I done?' she said out loud. Realisation suddenly hit her and she sat bolt upright in bed. What *had* she done? At this moment in time, she had no idea what she had actually done. Had she killed a man? Was he dead? Had he told someone what she had done before he died? She realised she had no idea what had happened after he had left.

It had only been 12 hours but it felt like an eternity. The telltale vibration of a voicemail dragged her back from her thoughts. She reached for her phone. One missed call - from him, from the man she stabbed with a kitchen knife. A very slight air of relief fell over her, as she realised that this meant that he wasn't dead and that she wasn't a murderer. Before she had a chance to exhale with relief, a sudden gush of panic blew across her. What did he want? What was he calling for? She pressed down on the keypad and held her breath as it connected to the message.

'Hi Emma. Err, just wanted to check you were OK? Can you call me back please? Nothing to worry about, just.. .well...just call me back. If that's OK. Please.'

Emma waited for the menu and pressed 7 to repeat the message. His voice was so soft that it was difficult to hear him. He said it was nothing to worry about. She sat for a moment taking it in. Then she sat for an hour, debating what she should do. If she wanted people to treat her like a grown up then she needed to act like one. Her mother had said that to her many times. Did she mean now? Is now the time she needs to act like a grown up?

It wasn't anything to worry about, he was right. He did just want to see if she was OK. He hadn't died. He hadn't been to the police. He'd just had a couple of stitches. He wanted to apologise if he had given off the wrong signals. He wanted to let her know that he still wanted to get to know her. He liked her. He found her intriguing. He suggested that they start again.

Emma sat at her kitchen table. The harsh fluorescent lighting bounded off the gleaming white surfaces. She sat at the kitchen table and smiled. He'd suggested they go for a coffee next time. And he'd meet her there.